Baby f

MW00881238

Tansy Dunn
illustrated by Janet Wolf

Dunn, Tansy.
Baby food.

ISBN 1 86388 599 4.

1. Readers (Primary). I. Wolf, Janet, 1957–.
II. Title. (Series: Reading discovery.)

428.6

Printed in Hong Kong.

9 8 7 6 5 4 3 2   789/9

SCHOLASTIC
SYDNEY AUCKLAND NEW YORK TORONTO LONDON

Food goes in.

Food comes out.

Spoon goes down.

Spoon comes up.

Bowl goes on.

Bowl comes off.

Baby comes out.